See Rock City
& Other Destinations

Scenic Route

Book and Lyrics by
Adam Mathias

Music by
Brad Alexander

A SAMUEL FRENCH ACTING EDITION

SAMUEL FRENCH

FOUNDED 1830

SAMUELFRENCH.COM
SAMUELFRENCH-LONDON.CO.UK

FOR PRODUCTION ENQUIRIES

UNITED STATES AND CANADA
Info@SamuelFrench.com
1-866-598-8449

UNITED KINGDOM AND EUROPE
Plays@SamuelFrench-London.co.uk
020-7255-4302

Each title is subject to availability from Samuel French, depending
upon country of performance. Please be aware that *SEE ROCK CITY
& OTHER DESTINATIONS – SCENIC ROUTE* may not be licensed by
Samuel French in your territory. Professional and amateur producers
should contact the nearest Samuel French office or licensing partner to
verify availability.

MUSIC USE NOTE

Licensees are solely responsible for obtaining formal written permission from copyright owners to use copyrighted music in the performance of this play and are strongly cautioned to do so. If no such permission is obtained by the licensee, then the licensee must use only original music that the licensee owns and controls. Licensees are solely responsible and liable for all music clearances and shall indemnify the copyright owners of the play(s) and their licensing agent, Samuel French, against any costs, expenses, losses and liabilities arising from the use of music by licensees. Please contact the appropriate music licensing authority in your territory for the rights to any incidental music.

RENTAL MATERIALS

An orchestration consisting of **Full Score, Piano/Vocal Score, Cello, Guitar,** and **Bass** will be loaned two months prior to the production only on the receipt of the Licensing Fee quoted for all performances, the rental fee, and a refundable deposit.

Please contact Samuel French for perusal of the music materials as well as a performance license application.

IMPORTANT BILLING AND CREDIT REQUIREMENTS

If you have obtained performance rights to this title, please refer to your licensing agreement for important billing and credit requirements.

SEE ROCK CITY & OTHER DESTINATIONS was originally developed and produced at Barrington Stage, Pittsfield, MA, Julianne Boyd, Artistic Director, and William Finn, Artistic Producer, Musical Theatre Lab in August 2008. The performance was directed by Kevin Del Aguila and music directed by Vadim Feichtner, with sets by Brian Prather, costumes by Mark Mariani, lighting by David F. Segal. The Production Stage Manager was Wesley Apfel. The cast was as follows:

JESS/CUTTER	Benjamin Schrader
DODI/LILY	Gwen Hollander
EVAN/RICK	Wesley Taylor
LAUREN/JUDY	Cassie Wooley
GRAMPY/CARNEY	John Jellison
DEMPSEY/TOUR GUIDE	David Rossmer
CLAIRE/KATE	Jill Abramovitz

The Off Broadway premiere of *SEE ROCK CITY & OTHER DESTINATIONS* was developed and produced by Transport Group Theatre Company, Jack Cummings, III, Artistic Director; Lori Fineman, Executive Director, at The Duke Theatre on 42nd Street in New York City, July and August 2010. The performance was directed by Jack Cummings III and music directed by Justin Hatchimonji, with sets and costumes by Dane Laffrey, lighting by R. Lee Kennedy and orchestrations by Justin Hatchimonji. The Stage Manager was Theresa Flanagan; the Production Manager, Wendy Patten. The cast was as follows:

JESS/CUTTER	Bryce Ryness
DODI/LILY	Mamie Parris
EVAN/RICK	Stanley Bahorek
LAUREN/JUDY	Sally Wilfert
GRAMPY/CARNEY	Ryan Hilliard
DEMPSEY/TOUR GUIDE	Jonathan Hammond
CLAIRE/KATE	Donna Lynne Champlin

From August 15 through August 21 the role of **JESS/CUTTER** was played by Nicholas Belton.

CHARACTERS

JESS – A twenty-something traveler. He's been on the road as long as he can remember.

DODI – A small-town Carolina waitress. She's never left the state.

EVAN – A twenty-something loner. No money, no girlfriend, no job...but he hasn't given up hope.

LAUREN – A thirty-year-old teacher from Fredericksburg. She's single.

GRAMPY – Lauren's beloved grandfather. He suffered a stroke a few years ago that left him unable to walk or speak.

DEMPSEY – A thirty-something professional. He's a divorce lawyer, but he hates it, if that makes it any better.

LILY – Judy and Claire's younger sister. She just wants her sisters to get along.

JUDY – Lily and Claire's sister. She's emotional.

CLAIRE – Lily and Judy's sister. She just wants to get this over with.

CUTTER – A prep-school teen. He's the "bad kid."

RICK – A prep-school teen. He's Cutter's best friend.

KATE – A bride. She's not ready...or is she?

TOUR GUIDE – A tour guide. He's determined to give Kate a little push.

WAITER

SUBWAY CONDUCTOR

FREAK SHOW BARKER

CARNEY

CHARACTER TRACKS

Man 1 Jess, Waiter, Cutter
Man 2 Evan, Rick
Man 3 Grampy, Subway Conductor/Barker/Carney
Man 4 Dempsey, Tour Guide
Woman 1 Dodi, Lily
Woman 2 Lauren, Judy
Woman 3 Claire, Kate

STAGE DIRECTIONS

Transport Group Theatre Company's original off-Broadway production, as directed by Jack Cummings III, incorporated spoken stage directions into the play. Each destination was "narrated" by a different actor. While this approach is not required, we find it adds to the unity of the various stories and reveals interesting connections. Spoken stage directions have been printed in **bold.** The scenes are assigned as follows:

Rock City - **CLAIRE/KATE**
33.39 N, 104.53 W - **DEMPSEY/TOUR GUIDE**
The Alamo - **DODI/LILY**
Glacier Bay - **GRAMPY**
Coney Island - **LAUREN/JUDY**
Niagara Falls - **JESS/CUTTER**
Finale - **CLAIRE/KATE**

EDITOR'S NOTE

The *Scenic Route* edition of *See Rock City & Other Destinations* is a school version of the original musical that has been adapted to be more community-friendly. Most of the original script remains unchanged with the exception of the Coney Island scene/songs. Much of the language in the Coney Island segment has been changed to suit more youthful audiences and performers. The original version contains a glossary of suggested terms that can be substituted in lieu of curse words; the "Scenic Route" edition applies these changes, making this musical an ideal choice for schools and other youth-based performing groups.

SONG LIST

Rock City
JESS, DODI
1. Rock City . . . . **JESS**
2. I Can Tell . . . . **DODI** & **JESS**
3. Mile After Mile. . . . . **DODI** & **JESS**

33.39 N, 104.53 W – 10:34 p.m.
EVAN
4. We Are Not Alone . . . . **EVAN**

The Alamo
LAUREN, GRAMPY, DEMPSEY
5. All There Is To Say. . . . .**LAUREN**
6. Grampy's Song. . . . . **GRAMPY**

33.39 N, 104.53 W – 2:15 a.m.
EVAN
7. We Are Not Alone (reprise) . . . . **EVAN**

Glacier Bay
LILY, JUDY, CLAIRE, WAITER
8. Three Fair Queens. . . . . **LILY, CLAIRE** & **JUDY**

33.39 N, 104.53 W – 4:06 a.m.
EVAN
9. Here . . . . **EVAN**

Coney Island
CUTTER, RICK, CONDUCTOR, BARKER, CARNEY
10. Q Train to Coney Island . . . . **CUTTER** & **RICK**
11. You Are My... . . . . **CUTTER** & **RICK**
12. Dark Ride. . . . . **CUTTER** & **RICK**

Niagara Falls
KATE, TOUR GUIDE, ENSEMBLE
14. Niagara Falls—the Tour . . . . **TOUR GUIDE, KATE** & **COMPANY**
15. What Am I Afraid Of? . . . . **KATE**
16. Some People Do/Finale . . . . **TOUR GUIDE, KATE** & **COMPANY**

0. OVERTURE

(The company enters, arriving at and en route to various destinations.)

DODI. It's not what I expected.

RICK. It's not too late.

DODI. Is it what you expected?

RICK. If we turn back now we could still make first period.

TOUR GUIDE. The tour's about to begin.

JESS. You ever feel like…there's gotta be someplace…

EVAN. They are coming.

JESS. …someplace you belong?

EVAN. They are coming here.

　　Tonight. I'm sure of it.

LAUREN. And, here we are…again.

CUTTER. What are you afraid of?

DODI. I want to see it.

DEMPSEY. It's hard not to feel patriotic.

KATE. I want to see it. I think.

CARNEY. Stay in the car.

　　Don't get out.

JUDY. All right.

CARNEY. No matter what.

JUDY. I'm ready now.

TOUR GUIDE. It's now or never.

DODI. So where you headed?

LAUREN. Did you hear the voice?

CLAIRE. Did you really think this was a good idea?

TOUR GUIDE. Wait until you see the view.

　　Amazing…

*(The company disperses leaving only **JESS** and **DODI**.)*

Rock City

(Late at night, in a diner, somewhere in the Carolinas,
JESS*, a twenty-something traveler sits, studying a large
highway map of the East Coast. He is the diner's only
customer. His waitress,* DODI*, watches him from the
counter. She wears a nametag that reads "Hi, I'm
Dodi!")*

(After a moment, she comes to his table.)

DODI. You haven't finished your dinner.

JESS. Oh, there's nothing wrong with it.

DODI. I know there's nothing wrong with it, but you haven't
finished it.

JESS. No. Guess I'm not that hungry.

DODI. *(overlapping)* 'Cause you looked hungry when you
came in.

JESS. It was a big portion.

DODI. Not really.

*(She waits. He looks up at her, then puts the map away
and eats.)*

You want some pie?

(Mouth full, he shakes his head, no.)

It's good. Maybe to take with you. It's good.

(He doesn't respond.)

So, where you headed this time of night?

*(He stares at her – can he tell her? Will she think he's
crazy?)*

What brings you through? Cause nobody's headed
here, I can tell you that. Everyone's going somewhere.
So where *you* headed?

JESS. Rock City.

DODI. Rock City? As in "See Rock City," Rock City?

JESS. That's the one.

DODI. Really?

> *(He nods.)*

> Why?

JESS. I saw the signs.

DODI. Sure, everyone's seen the signs – they're all over round here – if there's a barn, there's a "See Rock City" sign painted on its roof. What, you mean you *just now* saw the signs?

JESS. Just now.

DODI. Today.

> *(**DODI** waits for him to elaborate. Embarrassed, he looks down at his plate.)*

DODI. All-righty, then. You have a good night.

> *(She turns to go – he suddenly speaks up.)*

1. ROCK CITY

JESS.

> BEEN A LIFETIME DRIVING –
> NEVER KNEW WHERE
> I WAS HEADING.
> BEEN TRAVELING
> A LONELY ROAD.

> *(She turns back, intrigued.)*

> TILL TODAY, I'M DRIVING,
> AND I SEE THEM
> BY THE ROADSIDE;
> WHERE SILENTLY,
> THEY SPEAK TO ME...

> EACH BARN DECLARING A CLEAR DESTINATION
> SPELLS OUT A MESSAGE I CAN'T IGNORE.
> OUT THERE IT WAITS FOR ME,
> JUST OFF I-24:

> I'VE GOT TO SEE ROCK CITY,
> ANSWER TO EVERY PRAYER.
> COME ON AND SEE ROCK CITY!

JESS. *(cont.)*
> YOU CAN BE HAPPY THERE!
> EACH ROOF RECOMMENDS
> THE PLACE MY JOURNEY ENDS:
> ROCK CITY!
>
> SO I STOP AT A GASWAY,
> BUY A ROAD-MAP
> AND SOME JERKY,
> AND THEN I'M OFF –
> MY END IN SIGHT.
>
> SO INSTEAD OF NOWHERE,
> THERE IS SOMEWHERE
> I AM HEADING.
> I'LL SEE MY GOAL
> BY MORNING'S LIGHT.
>
> WITH EVERY BARN THAT I PASS I'M PERSUADED;
> AT EVERY ROOFTOP MY ROUTE REALIGNS.
> I'M DONE WITH MARKING TIME
> NOW THAT I'VE SEEN THE SIGNS:
>
> THEY SAY TO "SEE ROCK CITY!"
> IN LETTERS TEN FEET HIGH.
> I'VE GOT TO SEE ROCK CITY!
> WON'T LET THE CHANCE GO BY.
> CAN'T YOU FEEL THE THRILL?
> JUST FOUR MORE HOURS TILL:
> ROCK CITY…
>
> NOW AFTER YEARS ON THE HIGHWAY,
> I THINK I FINALLY SEE
> WHERE I'M MEANT TO BE.
>
> I'VE GOT TO SEE ROCK CITY.
> I CAN'T RESIST ITS CALL.
> YOU'VE GOT TO SEE ROCK CITY
> YOU'VE GOT TO SEE IT ALL.
> NO MORE MOVING ON
> AFTER THIS NIGHT IS THROUGH,
> FOR IN THE EARLY DAWN
> ROCK CITY WAITS FOR YOU.

JESS. *(cont.)*

> ROCK CITY!

> I-24 OFF I-59,
> EXIT ONE-SEVEN-EIGHT PAST THE GEORGIA LINE,
> GO LEFT AT THE LIGHT AND YOU'LL SEE THE SIGN:
> ROCK CITY!

DODI. Huh.

JESS. *(mortified)* God. I mean –

DODI. Wait right here.

> *(She exits suddenly. He gathers his things to leave.)*

JESS. Brilliant. Traumatize the wait staff.

> **(DODI** *returns, a duffle bag slung over her arm and a to-go container in her hand.)*

DODI. I'm ready.

JESS. What?

DODI. *(She is probably not as confident as she seems, but refuses to give in to the urge to turn back.)*

> To see Rock City. That's what you said, right? So let's go.

> *(She is heading out the door; he is fumbling with his money.)*

> Don't worry about the tip. Oh, and I brought pie.

> *(He leaves some money and follows her out the door.)*

(Somewhere along I-57 in his compact car – JESS in the driver's seat, DODI in the passenger's seat. They feign comfortability in silence.)

DODI. *(cheerily)* I'm Dodi.

JESS. Yeah. I know. You're still wearing your nametag.

DODI. *(reading her nametag)* "Hi!"

JESS. I'm Jess.

DODI. Oh, Okay.

(The silence returns.)

I don't usually get into cars with strangers, but well, you made such a sales pitch – and I got a feeling about you – a good feeling – and if I had to pour another cup of coffee I was just gonna kill somebody. I mean, not really. Just in my head, I mean. You ever kill somebody in your head? It's not very satisfying. Maybe this wasn't such a good idea.

JESS. You want a candy bar? There's one on the floor here somewhere.

DODI. No. No thanks. I think I'll wait for pie.

JESS. You want me to turn around? Take you back?

DODI. No! No. I want to see it.

JESS. No one's going to miss you? Wonder where you are?

DODI. I guess we'll see, won't we.

*(Yet another awkward silence. **DODI** pops open the glove compartment and starts sifting through its contents.)*

JESS. What are you doing?

DODI. I'm going through your glove compartment. You can tell a lot about a person from the contents of their glove compartment.

JESS. You can?

DODI. *I* can.

JESS. What can you tell?

2. I CAN TELL

DODI.

I CAN TELL...YOU LIKE COLLECTING THINGS:
PARKING TICKETS, MATCHBOOKS...DAY-OLD ONION RINGS.

(spoken)

You're going to be needing this receipt?

(She holds up a crumpled scrap of paper.)

JESS. Maybe... So, that's it?

DODI. *(continuing her search)* No...

I CAN TELL...YOU LIKE TO BE PREPARED:
FLASHLIGHT, CONDOMS...

(spoken)

Okay, now I'm scared.

(She pulls out a condom package.)

How old is this? It looks like it was made in 1984.

(He snatches it out of her hand.)

Oh look:

(She pulls a book out of the glove compartment.)

1984.

LITTLE THINGS TEND TO SAY A LOT:
A SEWING KIT.
A BAG OF POT.
I CAN TELL THAT THE THINGS YOU THOUGHT YOU KNEW
ABOUT YOU
AREN'T TRUE.

(She finds a photograph.)

(spoken)

Who's this? Your parents? They look sweet.

JESS. They were.

DODI. Oh.

*(**DODI** returns the contents of the glove compartment. An awkward silence.)*

JESS. *(trying to rekindle the conversation)* There's something *you* should know about *me*.

DODI. Oh?

JESS. I'm a psychic.

DODI. Is that so?

JESS. I don't even need a glove box.

DODI. Alright, let's hear.

JESS.

    I CAN TELL YOU'RE A BALLERINA.

DODI. Ha!

JESS.

    I CAN TELL YOU CAN ROLLER-SKATE.

DODI. No way!

JESS.

    I CAN TELL THAT YOU'VE NEVER LEFT THE STATE.

DODI. *(spoken)* Well, *that's* true.

JESS. *What?*

DODI. I've never left the state.

JESS. Never? So you've never seen New Orleans? Niagara Falls?

DODI. Nope.

JESS. Wow.

DODI. So, is that the best you can do, Mr. Mind-reader?

JESS. No. Um…

    I CAN TELL YOU'RE A PEOPLE PERSON.

    I CAN TELL IT WILL TAKE YOU FAR.

    HELL, IT ALREADY GOT YOU TO MY CAR.

DODI & JESS.

    AIN'T IT ODD, THOUGH WE'VE ONLY MET,

    HOW MUCH OF YOU

    I CLEARLY GET.

    DIDN'T KNOW YOU BEFORE AND YET SOMEHOW

    I KNOW

    YOU NOW.

DODI.

    I CAN TELL…YOU HAVE A CROOKED SMILE.

JESS.

> NO, I DON'T.

DODI.

> SURE YOU DO. IT KINDA FITS YOUR STYLE.

JESS. *(teasing her)*

> I TAKE IT BACK – CAUSE YOU SUCK WITH PEOPLE.
> YOU SHOULD HEAR HALF THE THINGS YOU SAY!
> BUT I GUESS I'LL FORGIVE YOU ANYWAY.

DODI & JESS.

> TWO HOURS IN AND WE'RE GOING STRONG.

JESS.

> YOU GOT ME PEGGED.

DODI.

> YOU GOT ME WRONG.

DODI & JESS.

> WHO'D HAVE GUESSED WE WOULD GET ALONG SO FAST?
> I JUST HOPE
> IT WILL LAST.
>
> I CAN TELL YOU SECRETS NO ONE KNOWS.

DODI.

> ONCE I WORE SHOULDER PADS.

JESS.

> I HAVE ELEVEN TOES.

DODI & JESS.

> THOUGH IT'S TRUE THAT WE'RE PERFECT STRANGERS
> STILL I FEEL THAT I KNOW YOU WELL
> THEN AGAIN, YOU MIGHT TRY TO KILL ME –
> WHO CAN TELL?
>
> *(A brief silence – not so awkward anymore.)*

DODI. So…Rock City.

JESS. Rock City.

DODI. What exactly *is* Rock City?

JESS. Well, it's a… It's…

> I don't know.

DODI. But you said –

JESS. I saw the signs.

DODI. Oh.

JESS. You ever feel like…there's gotta be *some*place…some-place you belong?

(*He looks at her. She doesn't respond.*)

Look. State line.

DODI. I think this calls for pie.

(*She climbs halfway into the backseat to retrieve the pie.*)

JESS. (*to himself*) I could get used to this.

DODI. (*pie container in hand, not having heard him*) What?

JESS. Did you bring forks?

(*She reveals plastic forks, opens the container and digs in.*)

DODI. Oh. This is good. Here.

(*She loads another fork and feeds a bite to him.*)

JESS. Mmm.

DODI. I know.

(*She is about to take another bite when something runs in front of the car. He stops the car suddenly, hitting the creature. They sit, stunned.*)

JESS. I think we hit something.

DODI. Ya think?

JESS. Should we check?

DODI. It might be hurt.

JESS. Right.

(*Finally, they work up the nerve to get out of the car. The only light comes from the stars and the car's headlights. In the darkness they find a large lump of an animal curled up in front of the fender.*)

DODI. Oh my god.

JESS. Is it dead? Did I kill it?

DODI. I can't tell.

JESS. What do we do? Well, don't touch it. Dodi!

(DODI carefully goes up to the creature and gives it a gentle nudge. It wakes suddenly and runs off, frightening the bejesus out of DODI and JESS. She jumps to his arms.)

DODI. Oh God!

JESS. Holy Jesus!

(after the shock wears off)

You saved it.

DODI. What?

JESS. It was dead and you touched it.

DODI. *(embarrassed)* It was not. I did not. I'm going back to the car.

(She goes to the car, then returns.)

I'm leaving it the pie.

(She leaves the pie container by the side of the road, and then returns to the passenger seat.)

JESS. *(quietly)* You saved it.

DODI. *(from the car)* Are we going, or not?

(He returns to the car and they drive.)

(Early in the morning, they have arrived at the entrance to Rock City. DODI sleeps in the passenger seat, while JESS surveys the area.)

(getting out of the car) Are we there? Why didn't you wake me? Is this it?

JESS. This is where it starts.

DODI. It's not what I expected. Is it what you expected?

JESS. I don't know what I expected.

DODI. I don't get it. How is this "Rock City?"

JESS. Maybe further up…

(They enter the park and begin to climb.)

(having reached a half-way vantage point…)

DODI. Oh, I get it. Rock. City. It's like a city of…

JESS. Yeah.

DODI. Where the rocks are like buildings…with streets and…

JESS. Yeah.

DODI. That's stupid. Besides, they're more like boulders than rocks. …Oh. I guess there's already someplace called "Boulder City."

JESS. Come on.

(They reach the summit.)

DODI. Oh. Wow. It's beautiful. Have you ever –

(finding a plaque)

Look at this. Look – look. See seven states from this spot. Georgia, Alabama…South Carolina…Have you ever seen anything so beautiful?

(JESS had been hoping to find answers, a destination, a meaning, something, anything…but all he sees is:)

JESS. The highways go on forever.

DODI. *(having not heard him)* What?

(He shakes his head, never mind – he can't take his eyes off the unending highways.)

Isn't it amazing. You can see everything. Everything…

3. MILE AFTER MILE

DODI.

> WIDE, WIDE,
> TOUCHING FOREVER,
> REACHING INTO ETERNITY.
> BOUNDLESS –
> NO LIMITATIONS,
> NO RESERVATIONS.
> I CAN SEE
> MILE AFTER MILE –
> ENDLESS SKY,
> ENDLESS VARIATION.
> NO END IN SIGHT –
> LIFE IS ALL AROUND,
> AND I FEEL I'VE FOUND
> HOME.

JESS.

> WHY CAN'T I SEE WHAT SHE CAN SEE?
> GOOD LORD, WHAT IS WRONG WITH ME?
> I FOOLED MYSELF TO THINK THAT I'D BE "ARRIVING."
> SHE SEES LIFE AROUND EVERY BEND;
> I SEE HIGHWAYS THAT NEVER END.
> GUESS THERE'S NOTHING LEFT FOR ME
> BUT MORE DRIVING.
> DRIVING
> MILE AFTER MILE –
> ENDLESS SKY,
> ENDLESS VARIATION.
> NO END IN SIGHT –
> I AM WAND'RING BLIND
> AND I'LL NEVER FIND

JESS.
A PLACE WHERE I CAN LAY MY HEAD,
JUST FREEWAYS AND PIKES INSTEAD.
THE HEADLIGHTS BLAZE
AND THE TRAFFIC IS THRONGING.
JUST ME AND MY CRAPPY CAR –
DAYS ARE LONG AND THE ROAD GOES
    FAR.
SO TO HELL WITH FINDING A SENSE
OF BELONGING.
LONGING
    MILE AFTER MILE –
    ENDLESS SKY,
    ENDLESS VARIATION.
    NO END IN SIGHT –
    AND FOREVER MORE
    I'LL BE TRAV'LING FOR

DODI.
GEORGIA,
SOUTH CAROLINA,
NORTH CAROLINA, TENNESSEE.

VIRGINIA,
AND ALABAMA,
EVEN KENTUCKY.
LIVING FREE.
I CAN SEE

    MILE AFTER MILE –
    ENDLESS SKY,
    ENDLESS VARIATION.
    NO END IN SIGHT –
    AND FOREVER MORE
    I'LL BE LOOKING FOR

BOTH.

    MILE AFTER MILE –
    AND I FLY
    TO THE VAST HORIZON WITH
    NO END IN SIGHT –
    EVERY BOUNDARY GONE,
    EVERY LINE WITHDRAWN,
    I KEEP GOING ON…
    FOREVER.

DODI. I am going to miss this. When I go back.

JESS. Back?

DODI. I have to do a double shift tomorrow. To make up for
    the day off.

JESS. I thought…maybe…

    (*He can't work up the nerve to ask her…*)

DODI. (*not hearing him*) What?

JESS. Nothing.

DODI. I can see my house from here.

    (***They scan the horizon*** *as the lights fade.*)

33.39 N, 104.53 W – 10:34 p.m.

(A vast, empty field at night – in the distance, perhaps, the lights of a military base. EVAN enters carrying a small stool, a pair of binoculars, assorted gadgets, and a video camera on a tripod. He sets up his stool and video camera, and then turns the camera on illuminating himself in its light.)

EVAN. *(to the camera)* July 5th, 2010*... Just outside Walker Air Force Base, Roswell, New Mexico. Time: Ten thirty-four. Skies: clear. Full moon, bright as can be. The fields themselves seem to be glowing. It was on a night like this, sixty-three* years ago, this very month, that first contact was made. My name: Evan Mann. And I am about to make a major discovery. You see, I've been tracking, for a while now, several...signs – indicators – of extraterrestrial life. Yes, UFOs. But these indicators – heightened static electricity, altered animal patterns, erratic barometer readings – all point to this date, this location – wait!

(He thinks he hears something and looks through his binoculars. He was mistaken.)

Not yet.

They are coming. They are coming here. Tonight. I'm sure of it.

4. WE ARE NOT ALONE

WORLDS
FAR FROM HERE
SEND THE MESSAGE: WE ARE NOT ALONE.

STRANGE
FREQUENCIES
KEEP REPEATING: WE ARE NOT ALONE.

I
GUARANTEE:
THERE CAN BE
NO DOUBT.

---

*Years can be adjusted to current or upcoming year.

EVAN. *(cont.)*

YOU
CAN'T IGNORE
THERE IS MORE
THAN JUST ONE PLANET CAPABLE OF HAVING LIFE
WHICH MEANS:
WE'RE NOT ALONE.

July 8th, 1947 the United States Military issues a press release that a "flying disc" – their language – has been recovered from this very field only some days before. A flying disc. Later they rescinded – took it back – claimed it was a "weather balloon." Weather balloon, my ankle. That was a flying saucer, a UFO, an alien encounter. The real deal. And you know what they say: lightning always strikes twice!

SOON
THEY'LL ARRIVE;
I WILL TELL THEM: "YOU ARE NOT ALONE."

THEY'LL
SPEAK TO ME
PROBABLY A LANGUAGE YET UNKNOWN.

(He stands to address the imaginary aliens.)

"I
COME IN PEACE –
WELL – WAIT IN PEACE,"
I'LL SAY.

THEY'LL
NOD TO ME
KNOWINGLY
AND I'LL HAVE CAUGHT IT ALL ON FILM TO
SHOW THE WORLD AND MY EX-GIRLFRIEND
I WAS RIGHT AND WE ARE NOT ALONE.

(to the camera)

I know what you're thinking. I don't mind.
CALL ME CRAZY!
YOU WOULDN'T BE THE FIRST.
I SWEAR I'VE HEARD IT ALL BEFORE.

(He looks through the binoculars.)

EVAN. *(cont.)*

    – IT DOESN'T FAZE ME.

    IF IT'S CRAZY
    THINKING THERE'S MORE TO LIFE
    THAN ONLY WHAT IS HERE ON EARTH,
    FINE: I'M CRAZY!

(forgetting the camera)

    I BELIEVE THE FUTURE LIES
    FAR BEYOND THESE LONELY SKIES –
    I BELIEVE IT MORE AND MORE EACH DAY!

    FROM ANOTHER GALAXY
    I HAVE HEARD THEM CALL TO ME;
    THEY'RE ON THEIR WAY!

NOW,
PRESENTLY,
ANY MOMENT THEY'LL MAKE THEMSELVES SHOWN.

JUST
WAIT AND SEE
ANY SECOND THEY'LL BE HERE;
OUT OF NOWHERE THEY'LL APPEAR.
DON'T YOU FEAR, CAUSE WE ARE NOT A
LOCALIZED PHENOMENON AND
FINALLY YOU'LL SEE: WE'RE NOT ALONE!
ALONE!
ALONE!

*(**EVAN** spots someone entering the far side of the field.)*

Hey! Hey! Find your own coordinates. These are taken.

(He goes off to get rid of the interloper.)

(blackout)

The Alamo

(A weekday afternoon at The Alamo. A lawyer in his thirties, DEMPSEY, sits on a park bench facing the fort. LAUREN enters, pushing her GRAMPY in his wheelchair. She regards the fort, while her GRAMPY feebly looks for someone he is expecting.)

(DEMPSEY notices them enter.)

LAUREN. And, here we are…again. Every year it looks smaller.

(GRAMPY mumbles something completely indiscernible, but LAUREN appears to understand.)

Yes, Grampy, you look smaller, too. But surrounded by all this…development.

(GRAMPY mumbles.)

How can you say it's the same? None of these chains had even been thought of when you first…

(GRAMPY again.)

The *Starbucks.*

(lovingly)

Of course you wouldn't be able to see them. What with your eyesight the way it is. I could probably have taken you to the local Jiffy-Lube and told you *that* was the Alamo…and we could have skipped this year all together. I remember – when we were little – when it wasn't a shopping mall… Ha! I "remember the Alamo."

(GRAMPY asks her a question.)

No, I don't see her. …I never do. As if I could.

(GRAMPY grumbles angrily at her.)

What's that supposed to mean? Don't start. We're not having this conversation again. I believe… I *believe*… This isn't about me – it's *your* anniversary.

(GRAMPY begins to become exasperated at not being able to fully communicate with her. LAUREN attempts to calm him down.)

Now don't get yourself upset. I know, I know…

5. ALL THERE IS TO SAY

LAUREN. *(cont.)*
I HEAR YOU, GRAMPY,
BELIEVE ME, I HEAR.
YOU DON'T HAVE TO WORRY,
I'M GETTING THE MESSAGE LOUD AND CLEAR.

YOU DON'T HAVE TO GRUMBLE;
YOU DON'T NEED TO SHOUT.
I KNOW EVERY SENTENCE YOU'RE TRYING TO GET OUT:

YOU'RE GONNA TELL ME I'M LONELY.
YOU'RE GONNA TELL ME I'M SAD.
YOU'RE GONNA TELL ME I'M MISSING OUT
ON THE THINGS YOU HAD.
  BUT I'M OKAY IN MY SINGLE BED
  AND I'M OKAY WITH THE NOVELS THAT I'VE READ.
  AND I WOULDN'T HAVE IT ANY OTHER WAY...
  AND THAT'S ALL THERE IS TO SAY.

(She feels she has made her point...until **GRAMPY** *sticks out his tongue and gives her a raspberry: "Pfft.")*

YOU'RE GONNA TELL ME I'M STUBBORN;
YOU'RE GONNA TELL ME I'M "BLIND".
YOU'RE GONNA SAY I PROTEST TOO MUCH,
BUT I DO NOTHING OF THE KIND.
  CAUSE I WON'T MISS WHAT I'VE NEVER KNOWN,
  AND I ENJOY EATING DINNER ON MY OWN.
  NO MAN USING UP THE MINUTES ON MY PHONE
  OR TURNING MY HAIR TO GREY,
  SO DON'T MAKE A BIG DISPLAY...
  THAT'S ALL THERE IS TO SAY.

I mean it, Grampy. Case closed. Don't give me that look!

(stamping her foot childishly)

I am a *grown woman!*
YES, I KNOW EVERY LOOK ON YOUR FACE
EVERY GESTURE AND EVERY SIGN
AND I KNOW YOU WANT ME TO BE A BRIDE
BUT I CANNOT FORCE WHAT I'VE NEVER FELT INSIDE
AND BELIEVE ME, GRAMPY, I'VE TRIED...

LAUREN. *(cont.)*
    YOU'RE GONNA CALL ME A YOUNGSTER!
    YOU'RE GONNA TELL ME TO WAIT!
    YOU'RE GONNA TELL ME TO NOT GIVE UP
    THAT EVEN THIRTY'S NOT TOO LATE.
      BUT I'VE BEEN WAITING FOR FAR TOO LONG,
      AND I'VE BEEN LISTENING BUT I NEVER HEARD THE SONG.
      AND I DON'T NEED VOICES FROM THE SKY
      OR KNIGHTS ON HORSES, BANNERS FLYING HIGH,
      SO DON'T LET IT CAUSE YOU ANY MORE DISMAY:
      I WON'T HAVE WHAT YOU AND GRAMM HAD – *HAVE* –
      AND THAT'S OKAY.

I need you to hear me, Grampy:

I'M GONNA BE OKAY.

(**GRAMPY** *relents, giving her a kind and understanding look.*)

AND THAT'S ALL THERE IS TO SAY.

(**GRAMPY** *begins to cough.* **LAUREN** *digs around in her purse.*)

Oh, now don't get over-excited. There's a handkerchief here somewhere. I'm sure she'll show up.

(**DEMPSEY** *jumps up to offer his handkerchief.*)

DEMPSEY. Here. I have a…handkerchief?

(**LAUREN** *looks up at him. He stands there holding out his handkerchief. She laughs quietly at the sight of his grand gesture, then takes the handkerchief.*)

LAUREN. Here, Grampy, don't contaminate the national treasure.

(*She talks to* **DEMPSEY** *absentmindedly.*)

He gets excited. He's an old man. Well –

DEMPSEY. Yes.

LAUREN. Obviously. He's my grandfather. My "Grampy."

DEMPSEY. You're lucky.

LAUREN. Yes. I am.

DEMPSEY. *(shouting at him)* You're feeling better now, Grampy?

LAUREN. Oh, he doesn't need you to –

DEMPSEY. Oh.

LAUREN. Thank you.

> *(***GRAMPY*** says something.)*

He wants to know your name.

DEMPSEY. Dempsey.

LAUREN. We don't know him, Grampy. His name is Dempsey. *Dempsey.*

> *(***GRAMPY*** responds. She laughs.)*

DEMPSEY. What. What did he say?

LAUREN. He said, "What kind of a name is Dempsey."

DEMPSEY. It's Irish.

LAUREN. I don't think that's what he meant.

DEMPSEY. Probably not. Well, it was nice to –

> *(***GRAMPY*** grabs **DEMPSEY**'s arm as he attempts to leave.)*

LAUREN. Grampy, what are you –

> *(***GRAMPY*** says something.)*

Grampy, he's a perfect stranger.

> *(***GRAMPY*** again.)*

He wants you to stay.

> *(***GRAMPY**, more persistent this time.)*

He wants you to meet her.

DEMPSEY. Who?

LAUREN. My grandmother. She's not actually coming. She's dead. She's been dead for… They met here. When they were kids. "Young adults." And they came back every year since. Until, well, a few years ago… But he still insists on coming. Every year. To see her. And to listen for the voice.

DEMPSEY. The voice?

LAUREN. Oh, did I not mention the voice? It all sounds so much more rational without the voice.

DEMPSEY. Well, you better tell me. He's not letting go.

LAUREN. It sounds crazy, but…the first time they met – sixty-some years ago, right on this spot – my grandparents heard…*claim* they heard this "voice." Singing.

DEMPSEY. Well, what did it say?

LAUREN. "This is the one you will love forever."

DEMPSEY. Wow.

LAUREN. Yeah.

DEMPSEY. That's really –

LAUREN. Crazy.

DEMPSEY. *(overlapping "Crazy")* Romantic. They were together their whole lives. Sixty-some years – that's fantastic.

LAUREN. It can be somewhat intimidating actually.

DEMPSEY. Yeah, I can imagine.

(**GRAMPY** *drops* **DEMPSEY**'s *arm*.)

LAUREN. He's seen her now. She's coming over. Now they'll talk.

DEMPSEY. Maybe we should give them some privacy.

(**DEMPSEY** *crosses to the bench, then looks back at* **LAUREN.** *She considers her options, figures what's-the-harm and joins him.*)

(*Lights shift to* **GRAMPY** *as he spots his wife.*)

GRAMPY. There you are…I see you.

6. GRAMPY'S SONG

LOOK AT MY SMILING GIRL;
YOU HAVEN'T CHANGED A BIT.
I CAN STILL SEE YOU STANDING NEAR THE LANDING
LOOKING LIKE A DREAM COME TRUE.
I REMEMBER…I REMEMBER…YOU.

I KNEW RIGHT FROM THE START
THAT WE WERE MEANT TO BE.
ON THAT FIRST DAY I TOLD YOU I WOULD HOLD YOU
AND I'D NEVER SET YOU FREE.
I REMEMBER…DO YOU REMEMBER…ME?

(Lights shift to where **DEMPSEY** *and* **LAUREN** *sit, staring at the fort.)*

DEMPSEY. It's hard not to feel patriotic. "The Alamo."

LAUREN. *(conversationally)* I read it's all a felonious cover-up for the mass murder of thousands of natives.

(realizing this may have been rude)

So, what brings you here?

DEMPSEY. I work in that building, there, behind the Starbucks. I'm a lawyer. I'm on lunch –

LAUREN. Oh really, what kind?

DEMPSEY. Sandwich…chips…

LAUREN. …of lawyer.

DEMPSEY. Oh. Divorce.

LAUREN. Oh.

DEMPSEY. Yeah. I hate it, if that makes it any better. What about you?

LAUREN. Salad, fruit-cup. I'm a teacher. In Fredericksburg.

DEMPSEY. Fredericksburg! That's not far.

LAUREN. No.

DEMPSEY. *(without thinking)* Do you have a husband? I mean…do you enjoy it? Teaching? Crap.

Listen: I'm just going to ask you if you're single and you can just answer me and then that will be all cleared up. I'm single. Are you?

*(**LAUREN** stares at him blankly – what has she gotten herself into?)*

(Lights shift to **GRAMPY**.*)*

GRAMPY.

TIME FLIES BY
TUMBLING INTO FOREVER
STILL OUR AFFAIR IS NEVER DONE.
YOU AND I
ARE ONE.

(*Lights shift to* **DEMPSEY** *and* **LAUREN**. *The conversation has gotten out of her control…*)

DEMPSEY. So, now that we've gotten that out of the way… Fredericksburg isn't really very far. And you're single. And I'm single. I don't have any kids. Do you have kids?

LAUREN. No.

DEMPSEY. I *want* kids. I'm getting ahead of myself. Is it just me or is it hot out here? I think maybe I'm having a sun-stroke.

LAUREN. I think maybe you are.

DEMPSEY. But, Listen…I saw you out here with your grandfather and thought…well…"She seems nice."

LAUREN. Ha! I mean, oh.

(**GRAMPY** *sings.*)

GRAMPY.
EVEN AS YEARS PASS ON,
WRINKLES ARE CREEPING IN.
DARLING I WON'T LET THEM REPLACE MY MEMORY
OF THAT DAY IN FORTY-FOUR…
I REMEMBER EVERYTHING AND MORE.

DEMPSEY. Anyway, I thought since we're both single…and don't have kids or live too far away…

LAUREN. Listen…you seem very nice –

DEMPSEY. Oh.

(*realizing it is not a compliment*)

Oh. I understand.

LAUREN. No, it's just that –

DEMPSEY. Is it because I'm a divorce lawyer?

LAUREN. It's not that.

DEMPSEY. (*noticing* **GRAMPY**'s *stillness*) Your grandfather.

LAUREN. (*confused*) No. What?

(*He points to her grandfather, staring motionless in his chair. She runs to his side.*)

LAUREN. Grampy?

> (**GRAMPY** *gestures to her to be quiet.*)

> You scared me.

> (*to* **DEMPSEY**)

> They're listening now. For the voice.

> (*They all listen for a moment. She wishes she could hear it. Nothing happens.*)

DEMPSEY. I should go. Tell your grandfather it was very nice to meet him...and his wife. They can keep the handkerchief.

LAUREN. It was...nice to meet you? Oh well. Good luck.

DEMPSEY. And to you.

> (*He begins to walk off, but pauses a few yards away.*)

LAUREN. To hell with it. Dempsey!

> (*She runs over to where* **DEMPSEY** *has stopped; we cannot hear their conversation. Suddenly,* **GRAMPY** *perks up. [Music underneath.]*)

GRAMPY. (*hearing the voice*) This is the one. This is the one you will love forever.

> (**LAUREN** *scribbles her number on a scrap of paper that* **DEMPSEY** *digs out of his pocket.* **DEMPSEY** *exits and* **LAUREN** *returns to her* **GRAMPY**. *She has cracked open the door to hope, but just as quickly closes it – this too, she is sure, will come to nothing.*)

LAUREN. Did you hear it, Grampy? Did you hear the voice? Well...maybe next year.

> (**She wheels him off** *and the lights fade.*)

33.39 N, 104.53 W – 2:15 a.m.

*(The same empty pasture. **EVAN** is back at his stool. The moon has shifted to another part of the sky. Coyotes howl in the distance.)*

7. WE ARE NOT ALONE (REPRISE)

EVAN.

NOW,

PRESENTLY,

ANY MOMENT THEY'LL MAKE THEMSELVES SHOWN –

TELLING US THAT WE ARE NOT ALONE…

(He catches himself yawning and turns on the video camera.)

Time: Two fifteen. No action yet, but very high readings of isotopic activity. The coyotes are going crazy. They know. They definitely know. This is it.

Wait until the guys back at the office see this. They'll want to hire me back so fast. And Amanda… Amanda, if you're watching…and you're watching…don't forget: you could have been here. You had you're chance. But *no*. You called me "*crazy*." You made me "*choose*." Well, I chose right. I chose –

(He looks through his binoculars and immediately sees something in the sky.)

Oh my god! Oh my – Oh –

ANY SECOND THEY'LL BE HERE!

OUT OF NOWHERE THEY'LL APPEAR!

DON'T YOU FEAR, CAUSE WE ARE NOT A –

(He realizes that he is mistaken and is deeply disappointed.)

Damn airplanes.

(to the camera)

You'll see, Amanda. You'll see.

(He waits patiently, occasionally looking through the binoculars. Eventually,)

EVAN. *(cont.)*

ANY MOMENT THEY'LL MAKE THEMSELVES SHOWN –
SPEAKING IN A LANGUAGE YET UNKNOWN –
TELLING US THAT WE ARE NOT ALONE.

(The lights fade as a coyote howls far away.)

Glacier Bay

(The deck of an Alaskan cruise liner in Glacier Bay, Alaska. LILY stands at the railing. Her sisters, CLAIRE [tidy and businesslike] & JUDY [unkempt and open-faced], sit in loungers nearby.)

LILY. *(happily)* Dad always loved these Glaciers. The ice. The sun. The way they are always changing.
These cruises were always my favorite. We were so happy.

JUDY. So happy.

CLAIRE. More or less.

LILY. So, I guess, now we say goodbye.

(LILY pulls a small green urn out of her beach bag. Her SISTERS gather around her, all the while keeping an eye out for others.)

Goodbye, Daddy.

CLAIRE. *(tapping the urn dismissively, more concerned with not getting caught)* Goodbye, Daddy.

JUDY. Good – Good – Excuse me. Don't – I – Sorry!

(JUDY, overcome with emotion, runs off sobbing. With CLAIRE on the lookout, LILY slips the urn back into her bag.)

CLAIRE. *(gesturing to where JUDY exited)* Great.

LILY. Be nice.

CLAIRE. What?

LILY. She's upset.

CLAIRE. It's been over a year, and she still wants us to hold each other and cry.

(pointing at the urn in the bag)

We should have dealt with *this* months ago.

LILY. Daddy wanted us to do it here.

CLAIRE. Of course he did. Glacier Bay. Daddy loved Glacier Bay. Ice. Nature. Whales. Wonderful.

LILY. Claire.

CLAIRE. Lily, you know I love you. But a whole week with her? Did you really think this was a good idea.

LILY. You promised.

CLAIRE. I know, but if she says "I'm sorry" one more time, I'm going to throw *her* over the railing.

LILY. She's not that bad.

CLAIRE. She's a mess. Here she comes.

(**JUDY** *returns, dabbing her eyes.*)

JUDY. I'm sorry. I don't know what came over me. All of a sudden, I just – I felt Daddy's presence.

CLAIRE. Daddy's gone, Judy.

JUDY. I know that. I'm not an idiot.

CLAIRE. That's not what I meant.

JUDY. Well, it sounded like what…

(*trying to avoid a fight*)

I'm sorry.

CLAIRE. Well, don't apologize.

JUDY. I'm sorry.

CLAIRE. *Don't* apologize.

JUDY. (*apologizing for apologizing, then apologizing for apologizing for apologizing*) Sorry. Sorry.

(*to* **LILY**, *almost whispering*)

Sorry.

CLAIRE. Let's get this over with. I'd rather not spend my vacation in "the brig."

(*They extend the urn over the railing, preparing to tip it.*)

LILY. Goodbye, Daddy.

CLAIRE. Goodbye, Daddy.

JUDY. Wait – I feel like I should say something. Dad – I – I don't know what to say. You say something, Claire.

(*She pushes the urn into* **CLAIRE**'s *hands.*)

CLAIRE. I don't need to.

LILY. Claire.

CLAIRE. Oh, all right. Dad was…a generous, loving father. He liked to laugh, and sing and write songs…And he loved glaciers. Done.

*(She hands the urn back to **LILY**.)*

JUDY. That's it?

CLAIRE. We did all this at the funeral.

JUDY. Don't you miss him?

CLAIRE. Of course, I miss him. But that's not him. That's a green jar from Home Depot.

JUDY. *(overlapping)* It's not just a jar, it's your father who raised you!

*(**LILY** returns the urn to her bag.)*

LILY. *(interrupting their spat)* Guys! Guys!

*(**CLAIRE** and **JUDY** stop fighting and return to their chairs. After an uncomfortable silence, **LILY** looks to the urn for help. Dad gives her an idea: she quietly sings the first line of "Three Fair Queens.")*

LILY.

THREE FAIR QUEENS OF THE NORTH ARE WE…

CLAIRE. Oh, no. No, no, no. How do you even remember that?

LILY. I remember all of Dad's songs.

JUDY. Which song was that?

LILY. The Glacier Bay song. Remember: I was Queen of the Frost. And you were Queen of the Snow.

CLAIRE. And I was Queen of the Ice.

JUDY. *That* sounds familiar…

CLAIRE. It should. He made us perform it for the whole ship.

LILY. You loved it!

CLAIRE. Ha!

8. THREE FAIR QUEENS

(a cappella throughout)

LILY.

>THREE FAIR QUEENS OF THE NORTH ARE WE
>RULING OVER THE FROZEN SEA
>EACH AS ROYAL AS QUEENS SHOULD BE
>SNOWFLAKES FLUTTER BY OUR DECREE

JUDY. *(remembering)* Oh, yeah.

LILY. *(to CLAIRE)* Second verse! Claire!

CLAIRE. That *won't* be happening.

LILY. *(goading her)*

>THREE FAIR QUEENS OF THE NORTH WE ARE...
>THREE FAIR QUEENS OF THE NORTH WE ARE...

CLAIRE. Oh for godsake,

>*(getting it over with quickly)*

>LIVING UNDER THE NORTHERN STAR
>HOSTING TRAVELERS FROM AFAR

CLAIRE & LILY.

>WE SELL TREATS AT THE QUEEN'S BAZAAR

CLAIRE. Great. Yay! Done.

(A moment later, JUDY finally remembers!)

JUDY. *(jumping up)*

>QUEENS OF THE TIGER'S WINTER LAIR

JUDY & LILY.

>QUEENS OF THE MIGHTY POLAR BEAR
>QUEENS WHO ARE WITHOUT...

ALL THREE.

>COMPARE!

(LILY pulls CLAIRE to her feet; she'll sing, but she refuses to dance.)

>THREE FAIR QUEENS OF THE NORTH WE SHINE
>SIPPING GLASSES OF SNOWFLAKE WINE
>EATING ICICLES OFF THE VINE

(They forget the words. CLAIRE takes the lead.)

>LA LA LA LIVE A LIFE DIVINE

LILY. *(gesturing to* **JUDY***)*
    ONE QUEEN TO SET THE SNOW TO FALL
JUDY. *(gesturing to* **CLAIRE***)*
    ONE QUEEN TO HOST THE PENGUIN BALL
ALL THREE.
    ONE QUEEN TO UNITE US ALL

(Giving **LILY** *a smack on the ass,* **CLAIRE** *joins in the choreography.* **JUDY** *surprises them with a high-pitched counterpoint.)*

CLAIRE & LILY.	**JUDY.**
THREE FAIR QUEENS OF THE	THREE FAIR QUEENS!
NORTH WE SING	THREE FAIR QUEENS!
DANCING ROUND IN A FAIRY RING	
LEGENDS TELL OF THE JOY WE	
BRING	
OUR ROYAL CREST IS A	
SNOWBIRD'S WING	

ALL THREE.
    SNOWFLAKES WILL FALL BY OUR DECREE
    DANCING UPON THE FROZEN SEA
    THREE QUEENS OF THE NORTH ARE WE!

(The **SISTERS** *finish the song and silently enjoy the rare camaraderie.)*

*(***JUDY** *is suddenly overcome with emotion and buries herself in her sisters' arms.* **CLAIRE** *pats her lovingly on the back.)*

JUDY. All right. I'm ready now.
CLAIRE. Let's do this thing.

*(***LILY** *retrieves the urn and they go to the railing.)*

LILY. Goodbye, Daddy.
CLAIRE. Goodbye, Daddy.
JUDY. Good –

(A **WAITER** *comes up behind them.)*

WAITER. Can I get you ladies anything?

(The **SISTERS** *quickly hide the urn behind their backs and huddle together.)*

CLAIRE. No.

LILY. No, thank you.

JUDY. We're so good.

(The **WAITER** *exits. The* **SISTERS** *remain frozen for a beat.)*

LILY. I think I just peed a little.

(They break into uncontrolled laughter. **CLAIRE** *and* **JUDY** *reenact the scene)*

JUDY. "Don't mind us, we're just dumping our father over the edge of the boat."

CLAIRE. "Great! Have fun with that!"

(They laugh some more.)

LILY. Dad would have loved this. Seeing us laugh. And sing. Why can't it be like this all the time?

JUDY. *(still laughing, throwing her arm around* **CLAIRE***)* Because Claire and I can't stand each other.

*(***CLAIRE** *and* **JUDY** *continue to chuckle.)*

LILY. Judy!

CLAIRE. It's true.

LILY. What's going to happen to us? Now that Dad's gone… we're orphans.

CLAIRE. We're grown ups. We'll still see each other.

JUDY. Of course we will.

(In the silence they look out at the passing glacier, none of them convinced.)

CLAIRE. Come on…let's dump Dad. Judy, say something sappy.

(They prepare to empty the urn. **JUDY** *thinks for a moment, then)*

JUDY. Even as the Glaciers continue to melt, shrinking smaller and drifting apart, their water replenishes the sea that connects them and ties them together.

CLAIRE. Way to romanticize global warming.

JUDY. Thanks.

LILY. Goodbye, Daddy.

CLAIRE. Goodbye, Daddy.

JUDY. Goodbye, Daddy.

> (*They pour the ashes over the edge of the ship* as the lights fade.)

33.39 N, 104.53 W – 4:06 a.m.

(The same empty pasture. EVAN *is still at his stool. He is deflated. **The moon is dropping below the horizon.**)*

EVAN. Time: Four o'six a.m. The coyotes have gone to sleep. No signs of…anything.

(He addresses the skies, quietly at first – then with growing agitation)

Come on. Come on! Come on!!

9. HERE

HOW COULD YOU PASS US BY?
HOW COULD YOU NOT DESCEND?
DIDN'T YOU EVEN TRY?
COULDN'T YOU COMPREHEND
  UP IN THE SKY
  YOU ARE MY ONLY FRIEND.
    FOUR O'EIGHT…
    STILL I WAIT
    HERE.

I GAVE UP ALL I HAD
JUST TO BE HERE TONIGHT.
EVERYONE CALLS ME MAD
THEN YOU GO AND PROVE THEM RIGHT!
  UP IN THE SKY
  NO SIGN OF YOU IN SIGHT.
    I CAME THROUGH…
    WHY AREN'T YOU
    HERE?

HERE,
IN THE MIDDLE OF THE MORNING,
IN THIS GODFORSAKEN PASTURE,
IN THIS GODFORSAKEN TOWN,
HERE,
WITH MY COFFEE AND MY CAMERA,
AND NO MONEY AND NO GIRLFRIEND…
HOW COULD I HAVE THOUGHT THAT YOU WERE EVER
    COMING DOWN
HERE?

EVAN. *(cont.)*

MAYBE IT'S ALL A HOAX!
MAYBE IT'S ALL A SHAM!
WAIT TILL I TELL MY FOLKS
JUST WHAT A FOOL I AM!
UP IN THE SKY
NOBODY GIVES A DAMN!
ALL IN VAIN…
I REMAIN
ALONE.

(Dejected, he returns to his stool.)

(to the camera)

Time: Four thirteen. This is Evan Mann. Signing off.

(He reaches toward the video camera then decisively turns it off. *He is only in near darkness for a moment when a blindingly bright beam of light shines down on him from above, accompanied by a loud, pulsing noise. Slowly* **EVAN** *looks up. His eyes widen and his jaw drops in amazement.)*

Hi!

(blackout)

Coney Island

(Q train to Coney Island; 9 a.m. on a Wednesday; late spring... Two teenage prep school boys – CUTTER and RICK – ride the train.)

(The boys have un-tucked and loosened their dress-code shirts and ties. CUTTER, who clearly thinks of himself as more dangerous than he is, stands eagerly at the pole. RICK sits nervously.)

ANNOUNCER. *(offstage)* Coney Island bound Q train. Next stop: Brighton Beach. Stand clear of the closing doors.

(The subway doors close with a clear "bing-bong.")

10. Q TRAIN TO CONEY ISLAND

CUTTER.
> Q TRAIN TO CONEY ISLAND –
> GONE AWOL, YOU AND ME!
> TAKE ME TO GO KART CITY,
> GET ME A ZEPOLLI!
>> SCREW HIGH SCHOOL.
>> SCREW HOMEWORK.
>> SCREW THE PTA!
>> HEY BROOKLYN: KISS MY ASS!

(He moons Brooklyn out the subway window.)

> FOUR STOPS TO CONEY ISLAND –
> WAIT TILL WE HIT THE STREET.
> WE'RE GONNA RULE THE BOARDWALK
> AND EVERYONE WE MEET –

ANNOUNCER. *(underneath)* Brighton Beach! This is Brighton Beach. Coney Island bound Q.

RICK. *(simultaneously)* It's not too late. If we turn back now we could still make first period.

ANNOUNCER. Stand clear of the closing doors.

CUTTER. Does wittle Wicky want to go back to homeroom?

RICK. Don't call me –

CUTTER.
> WHAT ARE YOU AFRAID OF?

(The subway doors close.)

RICK. They'll notice we're missing.

CUTTER.

SURE THEY'LL NOTICE *YOU* ARE MISSING
AND THEY'LL CALL IN THE MARINES.
DREDGE THE HUDSON, SEND OUT SEARCH DOGS,
STOP THE TRAFFIC OUT OF QUEENS.

PUT YOUR PICTURE IN THE PAPER,
HAVE THE COUNTRY SAY A PRAYER...
ME – THEY'LL NOTICE I AM MISSING AND NOBODY'LL CARE!

RICK. Up yours – I'm going back.

ANNOUNCER. *(underneath)* Ocean Parkway. Next stop: West 8th.

CUTTER.

WHAT ARE YOU AFRAID OF?

ANNOUNCER. *(underneath)* Stand clear of the closing doors.

(**RICK** *tries to leave;* **CUTTER** *grabs his arm.*)

(The train doors close.)

CUTTER.

AFRAID THEY'LL CALL YOUR MOMMY?
AFRAID YOU'LL GET DETENTION?
AFRAID YOU'LL WET YOUR PANTS?

(spoken)

Don't be such a sissy!

YOU WANNA PROVE YOU'RE MANLY?
WELL, BUDDY HERE'S YOUR CHANCE:

TAKE A CLOSE LOOK AT YOUR OPTIONS
AND DECIDE WHAT YOU SHOULD DO:
YOU COULD MAKE YOUR OWN DECISION
OR DO WHAT THEY TELL YOU TO.

YOU COULD RUN BACK HOME TO HIGH SCHOOL –
YOU'VE GOT CLASSES TO ATTEND.
OR – SPEND THE DAY AT CONEY ISLAND...
JUST ONE DAY AT CONEY ISLAND
WITH YOUR BEST FRIEND.

(**RICK** *is at the doors, ready to leave, but this stops him.*)

ANNOUNCER. This is West 8th. Next and last stop: Coney Island.

(The subway doors close. **RICK** *turns back to* **CUTTER.***)*

RICK.

ALL RIGHT THEN, CONEY ISLAND,
SHOW ME THE BEST YOU'VE GOT.
I EVEN MIGHT ENJOY IT –
LONG AS WE DON'T GET CAUGHT.

CUTTER.

NO TEACHERS.

RICK.

NO PARENTS.

BOTH.

NO ONE IN OUR WAY.

RICK.

HEY BROOKLYN:

BOTH.

KISS MY ASS!

WE'LL RIDE THE ROLLER COASTERS
AND BRAVE THE BUMPER CARS;
STAKE OUT THE BATTING CAGES,
SNEAK INTO TOPLESS BARS.
THE CYCLONE!
THE SCRAMBLER!
DENO'S WONDER WHEEL!
TILT-A-WHIRL – SHOOT THE FREAK!

AND WITH NO ONE HERE TO STOP US,
WE'LL BE WHO WE'RE MEANT TO BE.
NOT TWO PREPPY KIDS FROM DALTON
WHO SPEAK LATIN FLUENTLY.

WE'LL WREAK HAVOC ON THE MIDWAY –
SHOW THOSE BROOKLYNITES WHO'S BOSS!
WE'LL BE KINGS OF CONEY ISLAND –
FRICKIN' *ALL* OF CONEY ISLAND –

BOTH.

> Q TRAIN TO CONEY ISLAND
> NEXT STOP FOR CONEY ISLAND
> WE'LL TAKE ON CONEY ISLAND
> YOU AND ME!
> YOU AND ME!
> YOU AND ME!
> YOU AND ME!

ANNOUNCER. Last stop: Coney Island. Everybody off. Everyone must leave the train. Last stop. Stand clear of the closing –

> *(The subway doors close behind them. They run down to the street, but stop suddenly when they realize…)*

CUTTER. What the –

RICK. There's nobody here.

CUTTER. It's early.

RICK. There's nobody here.

CUTTER. Suck-monkeys!

RICK. It's closed. Coney Island is closed. Great plan…ass-face.

CUTTER. How was I supposed to know.

RICK. "Let's skip school and go to Coney Island."

CUTTER. It can't be closed.

RICK. It can't? Why not?

CUTTER. I said so. …So what it's closed. It can't all be closed. Look – there's people over there.

RICK. Those people are all homeless.

CUTTER. They prefer to be called "bums." Or "hobos."

RICK. Bite me.

CUTTER. Come on!

> *(CUTTER finds a row of fun-house mirrors…)*

Hey look – look at me: I'm fat.

> *(CUTTER sticks his gut out emphasizing the effects of the mirror. RICK looks over his shoulder – he can't look away from his own distorted reflection. CUTTER moves on to*

the next mirror and straightens up, sucking his gut in [this mirror clearly makes him look skinnier.] He moves on to the next mirror, meant to make him look shorter, and bends over sideways seeing how low he can get. He moves on to the final mirror and is transfixed – it is not clear whether this mirror is distorted to the extreme or not at all. They stare at their reflections.)

RICK. Let's go home.

CUTTER. No! I didn't come all the way out here to drag your pansy ass home.

ANNOUNCER. *(offstage)* Freak Show! Freak Show! Step Right Up.

CUTTER. See: I told you something would be open.

RICK. Doesn't look open.

ANNOUNCER. Step right up. Step right in. Coney Island's world famous Freak Show.

CUTTER. What are you afraid of?

*(The stage darkens. **RICK** and **CUTTER** are inside the freak show. As the **ANNOUNCER** continues, their faces are lit by the reflection of light from the various "exhibits.")*

ANNOUNCER. Ladies and gentlemen. Boys and girls. Behold: Freaks…from around the world.

From far Persia – the Unflinchable Man! See him hammer a nail right through the middle of his own palm without even a wince… Watch as he swallows broken glass…and yet smiles… Amazing! Bizarre! Shocking!

CUTTER. *(suggesting an adjective)* Gross.

ANNOUNCER. Now – feast your curious eyes on this startling anatomical wonder! Is it a man? Is it a woman? Is it a fish? Dare you look? Can you resist her siren song?

(We hear the Siren's song as the lights of the exhibits appear and disappear quickly now.)

Our unending menagerie: The Invisible girl! The Illustrated Man! The Escape Artist! The Fire Breather! Human curiosities! Far-fetched, perverted things! All freaks of nature!

ANNOUNCER. *(cont.)* And now, ladies and gentlemen… Girls and boys… Our feature performer. The prize of our freak-museum. Prepare yourself to witness the utter inhumanity, the shocking horror of –

*(The lights shift suddenly back to normal. The **BOYS** have left the Freak Show now, back out on the thoroughfare.)*

RICK. That was cracked out.

CUTTER. Let's get tattoos.

RICK. I'm going back to school.

CUTTER. Pansy.

RICK. Ass-face. So what are we gonna do?

CUTTER. "What are we gonna do?" "What are we gonna do?" Don't you get it? We can *do* whatever we *feel* like.

RICK. Which is?

*(**CUTTER** stares at him for a moment, then hauls off and punches him hard in the arm.)*

Ow! Whadya do that for?

CUTTER. I *felt* like it.

RICK. You mother –

*(**RICK** tries to hit him but ends up in a chokehold.)*

CUTTER. Say it. Say it!

RICK. *(giving in, saying it)* Gay uncle!

CUTTER. You bet your ass "gay uncle." There's something you gotta learn – and the sooner, the better:

11. YOU ARE MY…

IF I WANTED, I COULD TAKE YOU DOWN.
I COULD KICK YOUR ASS FROM HERE TO STATEN ISLAND.
I COULD MAKE YOUR LIFE A LIVING HELL.
I COULD. IT'S CLEAR.

I COULD BEAT YOU TILL YOU'RE BLACK AND BLUE;
TEAR YOUR PINKIES OFF AND SHOVE 'EM UP YOUR A-HOLE.
I COULD REARRANGE YOUR BALLS FOR YOU:
ONE HERE. ONE HERE.

CUTTER. *(cont.)*

    IT'LL WORK OUT FINE –
    IF YOU STAY IN LINE –
    JUST REMEMBER: YOUR ASS IS MINE!

      I AM YOUR MASTER AND YOU ARE MY WARD.
      YOU ARE MY MINION AND I AM YOUR LORD.
      I AM YOUR WARDEN AND YOU ARE MY SNITCH.
      OH-OH-OH,
      YOU ARE MY BITCH.

RICK.

    SO YOU THINK YOU'VE GOT THE UPPER HAND?
    DON'T FORGET, MY FRIEND, THAT TWO CAN PLAY AT THAT
      GAME.
    LET ME TELL YOU SO YOU'LL UNDERSTAND:
    I TOO CAN FIGHT.

CUTTER. Like how?

RICK.

    I COULD SELL THE GUYS YOUR TEDDY BEAR.

CUTTER. *(sarcastically)* Oh, no.

RICK.

    I COULD SHOW YOUR PARENTS HOW YOU PASSED YOUR
      MIDTERMS.

CUTTER. Hey!

RICK.

    I COULD TELL THE GIRLS YOUR UNDERWEAR
    IS TIGHT… AND WHITE.

    YOU THINK YOU'RE SO GREAT,
    BUT THERE'S SOME DEBATE –
    BETTER LET A MAN SET YOU STRAIGHT.

      I'M YOUR PIMP DADDY AND YOU ARE MY WHORE.
      YOU'RE LIKE THE OZONE AND I'M YOUR AL GORE.
      YOU NEED SOME SCHOOLING AND THAT IS MY NICHE.
      OH-OH-OH,
      YOU ARE MY BITCH.

CUTTER. I ain't no one's bitch.

RICK. Well, I'm not anybody's bitch, either.

CUTTER. Yeah… Except mine.

RICK. I ain't your bitch!

CUTTER. *(patronizing)*

> IT'S NOT SO TERRIBLE BEING MY BITCH.
> THERE'S LOTS OF THINGS YOU CAN DO:
> I LET MY BITCH HAVE PIZZA ON FRIDAYS;
> I TAKE MY BITCH TO THE ZOO.

RICK.

> I AIN'T YOUR BITCH, BITCH!
> YOU CAN TAKE YOUR ZOO AND SHOVE IT
> AND WHILE I'M THINKING OF IT
> *GET ME A GODDAMNED COTTON-CANDY, MOTHER-TRUCKER!*

CUTTER. Mother-trucker? *Mother-trucker??* Asswipe.

RICK. Bastard.

CUTTER. Dillweed.

RICK. Sucktard.

CUTTER. Panty-rag.

RICK. What-licker.

CUTTER. Snot-waffle.

RICK. Onanist.

BOTH. BITCH!

> I AM YOUR SATAN AND YOU ARE MY SPAWN.
> I AM YOUR JESUS AND YOU ARE MY JOHN.
> DON'T EVEN TEMPT ME, CAUSE I COULD GO ON…

CUTTER.

> AND ON…

RICK.

> AND ON…

CUTTER.

> AND ON…

RICK.

> AND ON…

BOTH.

> I AM YOUR BUDDHA AND YOU ARE MY TAO.
> I AM MUHAMMAD AND YOU ARE MY COW.
> I AM YOUR ELVIS (WITHOUT ALL THE KITSCH.)

CUTTER.

    YOU ARE MY –

RICK.

    YOU ARE MY –

CUTTER.

    YOU ARE MY –

BOTH.

    BIIIIIIIIIIIIIIITCH!

    II AM THE LEADER AND YOU ARE MY PACK.

    I AM YOUR DEALER AND YOU ARE MY CRACK.

RICK.

    I'M EPILEPTIC AND YOU ARE MY TWITCH.

CUTTER.

    I'M DENNIS THE MENACE AND YOU'RE RICHIE RICH.

RICK.

    I'M STANLEY KOWALSKI AND YOU'RE THAT GUY MITCH!

BOTH.

    AND YOU –

    (suddenly sweet and easy-listening)

    YOU ARE MY BITCH.

    *(****CUTTER**** sucker punches ****RICK**** in the gut. ****RICK**** doubles over in surprise and then the ****BOYS**** play-wrestle. Sound effects of the Spook House begin. ****CUTTER**** stops suddenly.)*

CUTTER. You hear that?

RICK. What?

CUTTER. *(developing a plan)* Huh.

RICK. What?

CUTTER. What we're gonna do. Less you're too scared.

RICK. I'm not too scared, ass-face.

CUTTER. Alright then. Let's go.

RICK. Where?

CUTTER. I thought you weren't scared.

RICK. I'm not. Where are we going?

CUTTER. Spook House.

RICK. The Spook House? You mean that stupid ride in the dark?

CUTTER. You can hold my hand if you want.

RICK. Why would we go on that stupid ride?

CUTTER. I don't know. Too scary for you?

RICK. No.

CUTTER. Alright then.

RICK. Alright then.

(*They approach the ride's entrance.*)

CUTTER. I'm getting tickets. Gimme a five.

RICK. Why?

CUTTER. Give me a five.

(**RICK** *hands him a five-dollar bill.* **CUTTER** *goes to buy the tickets and quickly returns.*)

RICK. (*referring to the offstage ticket-seller*) He's giving us weird looks.

CUTTER. He's got one eye.
Come on.

(***They go to the ride. A large, menacing* CARNEY *guards the entrance. A car, just big enough for two, pulls up.***)

CARNEY. Get in. And don't get out. No matter what.

CUTTER. Okay.

(*They get in the car.*)

CARNEY. Stay in the car.

RICK. Yeah, alright.

(*The* **CARNEY** *slams the car's door closed and the ride begins.*)

Ow. He's scarier than the ride.

CUTTER. I could take him.

RICK. With a stepladder.

CUTTER. Bite me.

(*The ride is very dark with occasional glimmers of light reflecting of the faux-gory exhibits.*)

RICK. It's dark in here.

CUTTER. Pansy.

RICK. Ass-face. I'm just saying.

CUTTER. That plastic skeleton is so scary. Hold me.

RICK. Hold yourself. Ew.

CUTTER. It's just corn-syrup.

RICK. I know it's just corn-syrup.

> *(They are in complete darkness.)*

Has the ride stopped? Are we moving?

CUTTER. I can't tell. I can't see anything.

> *(CUTTER jokingly flails around.)*

Are you there? I can't see you. Where are you?

RICK. Dude, stop it. Stop grabbing me. Dude – that's my dick.

CUTTER. I wondered what was so small.

RICK. Shut-up. Ass-face.

CUTTER. Pansy. Wait. Do you hear that?

RICK. What?

CUTTER. Shut up a second.

> *(They sit in silence. Suddenly, the CARNEY bursts through a door backed by bright, blinding sunlight; CUTTER, surprised, lets out a yelp.)*

CARNEY. Stay in the car!

> *(The CARNEY disappears as suddenly and the darkness returns.)*

CUTTER. Geez, man.

RICK. You screamed like a girl.

CUTTER. Shut up.

> *(Their sung lines are understood to be their thoughts.)*

12. DARK RIDE

RICK.

IS THAT HIS HAND?

CUTTER. How long do you think this is gonna take?

RICK. You got somewhere to go?

...AGAINST MY HAND?

CUTTER.	**RICK.**
I'M HOLDING HIS HAND.	
	I SHOULD BE IN ALGEBRA
HE'S NOT LETTING GO.	
	X IS THE SUBSET OF Y.
I'M FEELING HIS PULSE.	
	A SQUARED PLUS B SQUARED
	IS C SQUARED...
	IS HE SCARED?
I'M TOUCHING HIS THIGH.	
	I WAS SAFE BACK IN SCHOOL.
	I WAS SAFE IN THE LIGHT.
I FEEL...STRANGE.	
	I'M LOSING MY MIND.
STRANGE FEELS...GOOD.	
	HE'S MOVING HIS HAND.
DOES HE HATE ME?	
	I CAN'T GET MY BREATH.
WILL HE HATE ME?	
	I'M MOVING MY HAND.
HIS BREATH FEELS WARM	
AND HIS HAIR SMELLS FINE.	
AND HIS NECK TASTES DAMP	
AS HIS CHEEK BRUSHES MINE.	
AND I'M NOT HERE.	AND I'M NOT HERE.
BUT HE IS HERE	BUT HE IS HERE
AND WE ARE HERE.	AND WE ARE HERE.
	WE MOVE CLOSER,
	SHIFTING PLACES.
	LOSING TRACK,
	BUT LEAVING TRACES.

CUTTER.	RICK.
	HOLDING ON.
LETTING GO.	
WHILE SOMEHOW KNOWING	WHILE SOMEHOW KNOWING
I AM LOST.	I AM LOST.
I AM FOUND.	I AM FOUND.
I AM SAFE INSIDE THIS DARK,	I AM SAFE INSIDE THIS DARK,
DARK RIDE.	DARK RIDE.
WHAT HAPPENS NOW?	
	WHAT HAPPENS NOW?
NOW THAT I'VE TOUCHED	
HIM?	NOW THAT I'VE HELD HIM?
	WHAT DOES HE THINK?
WHAT DOES HE WANT?	
AM I SAFE IN THE DARK?	I
AM I SAFE IN THE LIGHT?	AM
	LOST.
DOES HE HATE ME?	
	WILL HE HATE ME?
I	IS HE THINKING
AM	WHAT I'M THINKING?
LOST	DOES HE FEEL THE SAME
INSIDE.	INSIDE?

(The ride ends: the car returning to the sunlight, the boys with their hands folded in their laps.)

CARNEY. Get out of the car!

(They leave the ride.)

CUTTER. That was lame.

RICK. Yeah. That wasn't scary at all. So – what do you want to do now?

CUTTER. I dunno…

RICK. Hey, I bet –

*(**RICK** walks up beside **CUTTER** and throws an arm around his shoulder. **CUTTER** pulls away angrily.)*

CUTTER. What are you –

RICK. What's your problem?

CUTTER. Nothing. Just stay away from –

    (as if nothing had happened)

    C'mon, let's go see if there are any other rides.

RICK. No.

CUTTER. Come on, Ricky.

RICK. No.

CUTTER. I'm warning you, Ricky.

RICK. You're warning me what?

    (**CUTTER** *stares him down, face to face.*)

CUTTER. You better not tell anybody –

RICK. What? Tell them what? That you're a –

    (**CUTTER** *hits* **RICK** *hard across the jaw, sending him to the ground.*)

CUTTER. Faggot.

    (**CUTTER** *turns to go, but is stopped by* **RICK**'s *voice.*)

RICK. *(pleadingly)* What are you afraid of?

    (**CUTTER** *is frozen in his tracks. Blackout.*)

Niagara Falls

([Immediately,] in the darkness a cell-phone rings several times.)

*(Lights rise on **KATE**, in her wedding dress, answering her cell-phone.)*

KATE. Hi, Mom! Everything's fine. I just stepped outside for a little air. All that pink was suffocating. Yes, I know I chose pink. Because I wanted pink. Because I still want pink. Because I love pink!

(She takes a deep breath.)

I just needed a minute to myself. Yes, Mom, I'm on my way to the chapel right now.

(She hangs up. To herself,)

Right now.

(She doesn't move. She sings,)

WHAT AM I AFRAID OF?

*(A **TOUR GUIDE** appears.)*

TOUR GUIDE. Step right up – the tour's about to begin. See Niagara Falls in all its splendor! See the awesome glory of nature untamed! See Canada.
No overlook overlooked. All questions answered.
Step right up: the tour starts here.

*(**KATE** hurries over to him.)*

KATE. A tour?

TOUR GUIDE. Shall we wait for your husband?

KATE. Oh, I don't... My... Um...

(after a moment)

A tour?

TOUR GUIDE. *(handing her a brochure with a smile)* Alright, then: A tour.

14. NIAGARA FALLS – THE TOUR

TOUR GUIDE. *(cont.)* *(grandly)*

Over ten thousand years ago, glaciers swept North America displacing mountains, rearranging valleys, and bringing together two great bodies – of water – to create one of the most powerful forces of nature on Earth. Since that time, this destination has been cherished by geologists, ecologists, paleontologists and, of course, lovers.

Prepare yourselves to witness the overwhelming power, the stunning beauty of…

NIAGARA FALLS –

THE RUSH OF FALLING WATERS.

NIAGARA FALLS –

THE CLEANSING AIR.

HEAR HOW IT CALLS –

NO OTHER DESTINATION

CAN COMPARE.

Follow me; we're almost to Niagara's famous "Romance Gardens."

(as he leads her toward the gardens)

A favorite of honeymooners, these immaculate gardens were originally planted over one hundred years ago. Questions?

KATE.

IS IT WORTH A TRIP?

TOUR GUIDE. Thousands of flowers in hundreds of varieties.

KATE.

ALL THERE ON DISPLAY?

TOUR GUIDE. Not to be missed. Sublime!

KATE.

COULD IT REALLY BE

(The **TOUR GUIDE** *looks around, unable to find the garden.)*

AS PERFECT AS YOU SAY?

TOUR GUIDE. *(remembering)* Oh, yeah:
>LAST FRIDAY A TORNADO CAME AND BLEW IT ALL AWAY.

KATE. Wait – What?!

>*(A **CHORUS** of voices joins underneath.)*

TOUR GUIDE.
>NIAGARA FALLS –
>A GRAND RETURN TO EDEN!
>NIAGARA FALLS –
>UNENDING BLISS!
>HEAR HOW IT CALLS –
>NO OTHER PLACE ON EARTH
>IS QUITE LIKE THIS.

>*(**KATE**'s cell-phone rings with a different, distinctive ring-tone.)*

KATE. Excuse me.

>*(She answers her phone.)*

Daddy, now's not a good time. I gave them to Ryan, Jeff's best man. No, the other best man…the British one.

>*(She notices the **TOUR GUIDE** looking at her.)*

Gotta go, Daddy – lots to do! Getting ready! What?

>*(suddenly very sincere)*

I do love him. I really do.

>*(nervous again)*

Bye!

>*(She hangs up the phone. To the **TOUR GUIDE**, almost whispering [a la **JUDY** in Glacier Bay])*

Sorry!

TOUR GUIDE. Moving on.

>*(She follows him.)*

Coming up on our right: The Chateau de L'Amour! Famous for its rustic charm, the world-renowned hotel was built in 1916 and has been host to over a million newlyweds.

KATE.

    ALL THOSE HAPPY GUESTS.

TOUR GUIDE. So happy.

KATE.

    NO WONDER IT'S RENOWNED.

TOUR GUIDE. *(correcting her) World* renowned.

KATE.

    OVER NINETY YEARS
    AND YET IT'S STILL AROUND...

TOUR GUIDE.

    AN ARSONIST GREW FOND OF IT
    AND BURNED IT TO THE GROUND.

    (The Chateau comes in to view; **KATE** *is alarmed by its state.)*

    NIAGARA FALLS –
    THE GLOW OF BURNING EMBERS!
    NIAGARA FALLS –

KATE. Wait a minute, wait a minute. I'm sorry to interrupt, but doesn't this tour include anyplace that's *not* destroyed?

TOUR GUIDE. You're not satisfied?

KATE. It's not that. It's just – I mean: Niagara Falls...what happened to "romance," "beauty," "honeymoon capital of the world," "happily ever after"?

TOUR GUIDE. Haven't you heard? Times are tough.

KATE. But surely there must be something...

    (She scans the brochure looking for other options.)

KATE.

    CAVERN OF THE WINDS?

TOUR GUIDE. Besieged by wolves.

KATE.

    CHAPEL ON THE LAKE?

TOUR GUIDE. Chapel *in* the lake.

KATE.

    OBSERVATION TOWER?

TOUR GUIDE. Not so much.

KATE.

AMISH MARKET?

TOUR GUIDE. Closed.

KATE.

SCENIC TROLLEY?

TOUR GUIDE. Crashed.

KATE.

WAX MUSEUM?

TOUR GUIDE.

MELTED!

(He snaps the brochure from her hands and continues on his way; she follows him.)

TOUR GUIDE.	**KATE.**
NIAGARA FALLS –	Hey! Wait!
YOU'RE SUCH A WORLD OF	
WONDERS!	
NIAGARA FALLS –	
NIAGARA FALLS –	IS THIS ALL THERE IS?
THE RUSH OF FALLING WATERS.	IS THIS WHAT'S IN STORE?
NIAGARA FALLS –	SHOW ME SOMETHING ELSE!
A NAT'RAL HIGH!	SHOW ME SOMETHING MORE!
AND WHEN IT CALLS,	PLEASE, JUST TRY!
YOU HAVE TO SEE IT ONCE BE-	
FORE	BEFORE I –
YOU –	BEFORE I –

*(**KATE**'s cell-phone rings – the ring-tone is "Here Comes The Bride." She stares at the phone, but does not answer it.)*

KATE. Jeff.

TOUR GUIDE. Aren't you going to answer that?

Could be important.

(She stares at the phone, unsure what to do. The phone stops ringing.)

KATE. *(after a deep breath)* Okay, let's go.

TOUR GUIDE. Go where?

KATE. On with the tour.

TOUR GUIDE. The tour's over.

KATE. What? No!

TOUR GUIDE. Enjoy the gift shop.

KATE. That's it?

TOUR GUIDE. You expected more? It's just a tour, lady.
Let me guess: You were looking for a sign. A great
big symbol. Something to tell you: "Go ahead. It's all
going to work out perfectly."

Sorry, not part of the package.

(He starts to leave.)

KATE. There must be something you could show me.
Please.

(He stops in his tracks.)

I'm asking for your help.

TOUR GUIDE. I suppose, there is one other thing I could
show you…but I warn you – it's not for the faint of
heart.

KATE. Okay.

TOUR GUIDE. Strictly off the books.

KATE. Okay.

TOUR GUIDE. You can't tell anyone.

KATE. Okay.

TOUR GUIDE. *(whispering)* Lover's Leap.

KATE. Lover's Leap?

TOUR GUIDE. *(grandly)* Lover's Leap!

(He gives her back the brochure. She looks through it.)

KATE. Ah: "Lovers' Leap. The highest point in all of Niagara. Overlooking the widest and highest fall. Only for
the stout of heart." Huh: "Someone dies here every
year."

TOUR GUIDE. Huh.

KATE. Is it true? Someone dies here every year?

TOUR GUIDE. Yes. And this could be your year.

KATE. What?

TOUR GUIDE. But, if you don't want to see it…

KATE. No! I want to see it. I think.

TOUR GUIDE. Very well. Very well. Follow me.

> (*He retrieves the brochure, balls it up and tosses it away.* ***They go off the path and begin to climb.***)

Watch your step; wouldn't want to trip and kill yourself.

> (***They are engulfed in a thick mysterious fog.***)

Tada!

KATE. This is it? I can't really see anything.

TOUR GUIDE. Well, this isn't "it," per se. This is where you "get on."

KATE. Ooo, you mean there's a ride?

TOUR GUIDE. Sort of:

You see that barrel?

> (*The* **TOUR GUIDE** *points to a spot downstage.*)

> (**KATE** *stands, frozen. He can't mean what she thinks he means. She looks at the barrel; she looks at him.*)

KATE. You're not a tour guide at all!

TOUR GUIDE. Of course I am. You want a tour guide, you get a tour guide. Welcome to the tour!

KATE. You drag me all over creation. We haven't even seen a single waterfall.

TOUR GUIDE. You have someplace better to be?

KATE. (*ignoring his comment*) And then – And then – A barrel?! That's madness!

TOUR GUIDE. Yes. But wait until you see the view. Amazing. And the thrill of going over the edge – there's nothing like it.

KATE. You mean, you've done this?

TOUR GUIDE. This isn't about me, *Kate.* It's about you.

KATE. *(She stares at the barrel trying to make up her mind.)*
Nope. No. No. Not gonna do it.

(She starts to leave.)

TOUR GUIDE. Okay, then. Have it your way: Tour's over. Go
home.

KATE. Home?

TOUR GUIDE. Bye now.

KATE. *(turning back to him)* I want to see it.

TOUR GUIDE. If you want to see it, you have to get in the
barrel. Come on, Kate! What are you afraid of?

KATE. What am I afraid of?

15. WHAT AM I AFRAID OF?

WHAT AM I AFRAID OF?!

WHAT IF I START TO DRIFT
FAR FROM THE SHORE?
WHAT IF THE BARREL CRACKS?
THEN WHAT'S IN STORE?
WHAT IF THE AIR RUNS OUT?
WHAT IF I'M RIGHT TO DOUBT?
THAT'S WHAT I'M AFRAID OF!

*(The **TOUR GUIDE** shrugs, unimpressed.)*

WHAT IF I HIT THE ROCKS
AFTER THE DIVE?
WHAT IF I START TO SINK?
WILL I SURVIVE?
WHAT IF I LOSE MY MIND
ONCE I HAVE BEEN CONFINED
BARELY ALIVE!

I'M NOT READY
TO TAKE THIS LEAP.
NO, I'M NOT READY...
OR AM I READY?

*(She moves tentatively toward the barrel, then pulls back
suddenly.)*

WHAT IF I LOSE MY WAY?

KATE. *(cont.)*

  WHAT IF THERE'S HELL TO PAY?
  WHAT IF I'VE BEEN
  RIGHT ALL ALONG?
  BUT WHAT IF I'M WRONG?
  WHAT IF I'M WRONG?!

  WHAT IF THE THINGS I CHOOSE AREN'T THE THINGS I
    NEED?
  WHAT IF THE LIFE I WANT ISN'T THE LIFE I LEAD?
  WHAT IF WHAT IF WHAT IF WHAT IF –

  THAT'S WHAT I'M AFRAID OF!

TOUR GUIDE. Wow, lady… You've got issues.

KATE. I know.

TOUR GUIDE. No, I mean *major* issues.

KATE. I know.

TOUR GUIDE. So, what are you going to do about it?

  (Her cell phone rings: "Here Comes the Bride." She stares at the phone, as frightened as ever.)

  (The **TOUR GUIDE** *grabs the ringing phone from her hand and chucks it over the edge of the falls.)*

KATE. Jeff!

  (She watches the phone disappear, never having wanted it more. She turns back to the **TOUR GUIDE***.)*

TOUR GUIDE. *(shouting at her)* You think you're the only one who's ever felt this way? You think other people aren't afraid? Everyone's afraid, Kate!

  (suddenly real)

  Everyone's afraid. Afraid to be alone. Afraid to not be alone. Afraid of where they're going. Afraid of where they are. You've been given a chance, Kate. A chance to see something that not everybody gets to see. And you're going to turn your back on that, because you're scared?

KATE. I'm not ready.

TOUR GUIDE. It's now or never.

KATE. I'm afraid.

TOUR GUIDE. We've been through this.

KATE. What am I supposed to do?

TOUR GUIDE. Make a decision. You know you want to.

16. SOME PEOPLE DO/FINALE

OUT ON THE EDGE
TAKING THE FALL
MAKING THE CHOICE
RISKING IT ALL
THE ODDS MAY BE SLIM
THAT THEY'LL MAKE IT THROUGH
EVEN SO – SOME PEOPLE DO.

SOMETIMES THEY CRASH
TORN LIMB FROM LIMB
SOMETIMES THEY DROWN
UNABLE TO SWIM
PROVIDENCE SPARES
ONLY A FEW
MOST DON'T FLOAT – SOME PEOPLE DO.

WHAT ARE YOU WAITING FOR?

KATE.

WHAT IF IT ALL ENDS BADLY?
WHAT IF I WASN'T MEANT TO GO?

TOUR GUIDE.

YOU COULD BE RIGHT –
OR YOU COULD BE MISTAKEN.
IF YOU DON'T TRY YOU'LL NEVER KNOW.

BOTH.

TAKING A STEP
TAKING A STAND
HOLDING YOUR BREATH
HOPING FOR LAND
WELL, SOME PEOPLE FELL,
BUT SOME PEOPLE GREW.
IN THE END –

TOUR GUIDE.

IT COULD BE YOU.

(*KATE steps forward as the* **TOUR GUIDE** *disappears into the mist.*)

KATE.

NIAGARA FALLS –
I HEAR YOUR RUSHING WATERS
CALLING ME OUT
INTO THE BLUE.
BUT DO I DARE
TO CHOOSE TO TAKE THE CHANCE?

(*She makes up her mind, stepping forward.*)

I DO!
I DO!
I DO!

(*The fog clears –* **KATE** *is surrounded by the rest of the company.*)

LAUREN.

I DO!

JESS.

I DO!

DODI.

I DO!

RICK.

I DO!

ALL.

I DO!

(*One by one the actors exit leaving only* **JESS & DODI**, *as they were at the end of their scene. The underscoring shifts to "Mile After Mile."*)

DODI. (*filling the awkward silence*) Well…we've seen it. Rock City.

JESS. Yeah.

DODI. So, now what?

JESS. I'll take you back, I guess. Unless…

I hear there are these amazing caverns in Kentucky… this place called Mammoth Cave. Stalactites as far as the eye can see…

(nervously)

If you want…to see them…

DODI. Okay.

JESS. *(He looks at her for the first time in the conversation.)* Yeah?

DODI. Yeah.

JESS. Okay.

(They both look at the view, unable to hide their giddiness. Maybe JESS has found what he's looking for after all.)

Okay.

(They look out over the horizon.)

(blackout)

SAMUEL FRENCH STAFF

Nate Collins
President

Ken Dingledine
Director of Operations,
Vice President

Bruce Lazarus
Executive Director,
General Counsel

Rita Maté
Director of Finance

ACCOUNTING

Lori Thimsen | Director of Licensing Compliance
Nehal Kumar | Senior Accounting Associate
Helena Mezzina | Royalty Administration
Glenn Halcomb | Royalty Administration
Jessica Zheng | Accounts Receivable
Andy Lian | Accounts Payable
Charlie Sou | Accounting Associate
Joann Mannello | Orders Administrator

CUSTOMER SERVICE AND LICENSING

Brad Lohrenz | Director of Licensing Development
Laura Lindson | Licensing Services Manager
Kim Rogers | Theatrical Specialist
Matthew Akers | Theatrical Specialist
Ashley Byrne | Theatrical Specialist
Jennifer Carter | Theatrical Specialist
Annette Storckman | Theatrical Specialist
Dyan Flores | Theatrical Specialist
Sarah Weber | Theatrical Specialist
Nicholas Dawson | Theatrical Specialist
Andrew Clarke | Theatrical Specialist
David Kimple | Theatrical Specialist

EDITORIAL

Amy Rose Marsh | Literary Manager
Ben Coleman | Editorial Associate
Caitlin Bartow | Assistant to the Executive Director

MARKETING

Abbie Van Nostrand | Director of Corporate
Communications
Ryan Pointer | Marketing Manager
Courtney Kochuba | Marketing Associate

PUBLICATIONS AND PRODUCT DEVELOPMENT

Joe Ferreira | Product Development Manager
David Geer | Publications Manager
Charlyn Brea | Publications Associate
Tyler Mullen | Publications Associate
Derek P. Hassler | Musical Products Coordinator
Zachary Orts | Musical Materials Coordinator

OPERATIONS

Casey McLain | Operations Supervisor
Elizabeth Minski | Office Coordinator, Reception
Coryn Carson | Office Coordinator, Reception

SAMUEL FRENCH BOOKSHOP (LOS ANGELES)

Joyce Mehess | Bookstore Manager
Cory DeLair | Bookstore Buyer
Jennifer Palumbo | Bookstore Order Dept. Manager
Sonya Wallace | Bookstore Associate
Tim Coultas | Bookstore Associate
Alfred Contreras | Shipping & Receiving

LONDON OFFICE

Felicity Barks | Rights & Contracts Associate
Steve Blacker | Bookshop Associate
David Bray | Customer Services Associate
Zena Choi | Professional Licensing Associate
Robert Cooke | Assistant Buyer
Stephanie Dawson | Amateur Licensing Associate
Simon Ellison | Retail Sales Manager
Jason Felix | Royalty Administration
Susan Griffiths | Amateur Licensing Associate
Robert Hamilton | Amateur Licensing Associate
Lucy Hume | Publications Manager
Nasir Khan | Management Accountant
Simon Magniti | Royalty Administration
Louise Mappley | Amateur Licensing Associate
James Nicolau | Despatch Associate
Martin Phillips | Librarian
Zubayed Rahman | Despatch Associate
Steve Sanderson | Royalty Administration Supervisor
Douglas Schatz | Acting Executive Director
Roger Sheppard | I.T. Manager
Panos Panayi | Company Accountant
Peter Smith | Amateur Licensing Associate
Garry Spratley | Customer Service Manager
David Webster | UK Operations Director